D1592362

Hi, GUYS! I'm sure glad you were able to come over to play today.

This book belongs to:

RAYleigh WAller

**Created & Written by
Sarah Beliza Tucker
Illustrated by Adam Ihle**

Library of Congress Control Number: 2021906479

To reach Ocean Aire Productions, Inc. visit: www.AdventuresofHarryandFriends.com

This is a Black Belt Principles Series: Book Seven
Created & Written by Sarah Beliza Tucker- Illustrated by Adam Ihle

ISBN Hardcover: 978-1-953979-08-7
ISBN Paperback: 978-1-953979-09-4
ISBN Digital: 978-1-953979-10-0

Do you smell that!?!

Mom made COOKIES!
Let's GO!

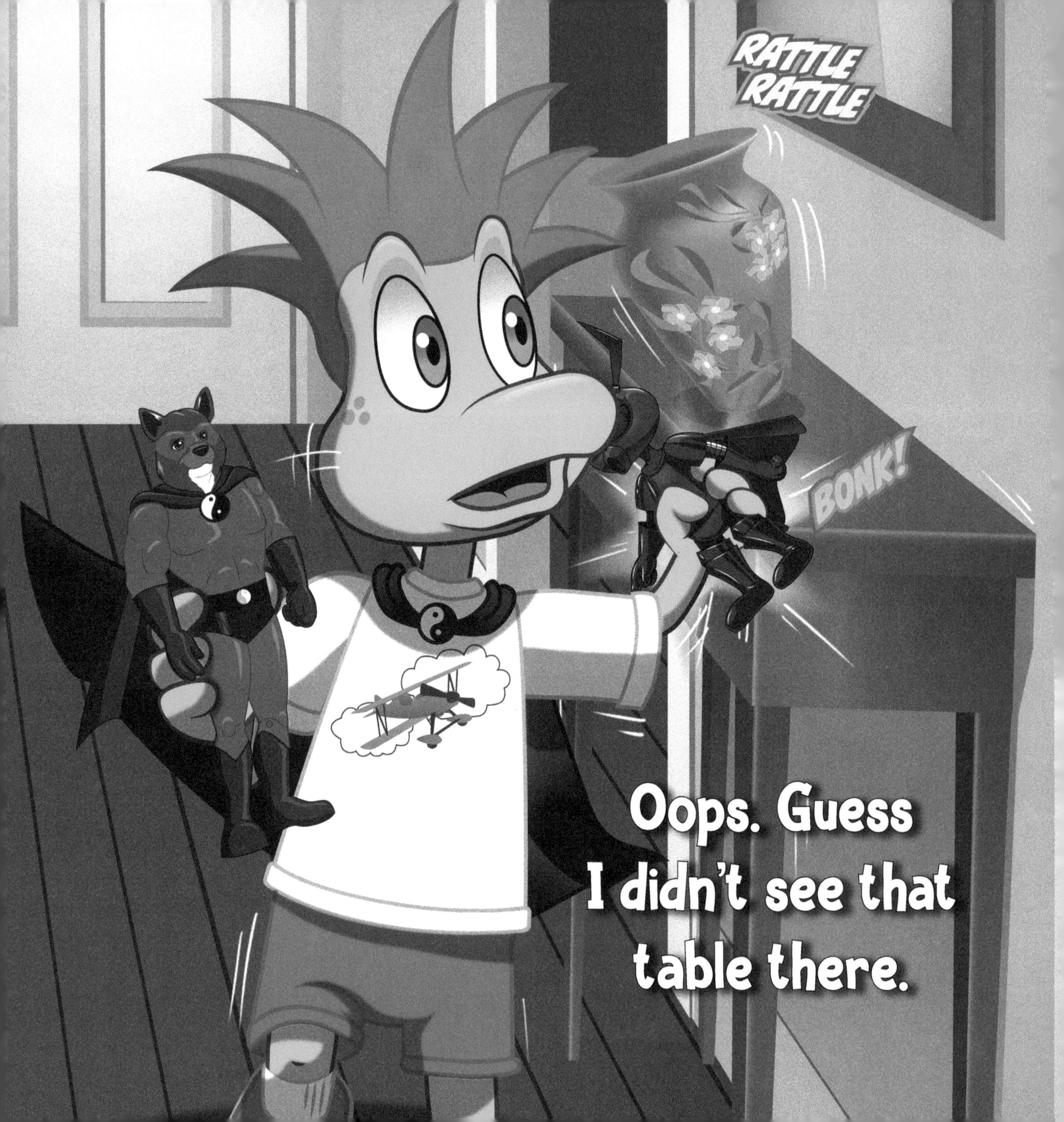

Oops. Guess
I didn't see that
table there.

Did you hear that?
Mom wants to know if
everything's okay.
But it's NOT!
What am I
going to do?

NOW HEAR ME OUT. IT'S TRUE. I'VE GOTTEN OUT OF MANY STICKY SITUATIONS BY BLAMING MY BAND OF NINJA CATS. THEY DO LOVE TO TAKE THE FALL FOR ME IF I'M EVER CAUGHT.

WHICH IS ALL THE TIME.

POOF!

POOF!

POOF!

I DON'T THINK I COULD BLAME SOMEONE ELSE FOR THIS. I DON'T WANT MY FRIENDS TO GET IN TROUBLE.

WHICH IS WHY YOU SHOULD TELL THE TRUTH.

Hmmm...Should I lie? Or should I tell her the truth?

Harry's heart pounds in his chest, as he blurts out, **"IT'S ALL MY FAULT**, no one else's. I smelled your cookies, and I was so excited that I ran out of my room...and into the table. That's when your favorite vase fell."

He swallows loudly, then says, "The Black Beetle said I should tell you a story to get out of trouble, but Captain Karate Man said I should tell the truth no matter the consequences. He told me that if I lie, I could lose your trust, and that would be even worse."

"Sooo...I'm ready for any punishment you see fit. Even if it's jail time. I deserve it."

Harry's mom just stands there, looking at him. She doesn't say a word. As she turns and walks away, Harry's stomach twists into knots, and he says, "Where is she going? What if she's planning a punishment even worse than jail? I'm in so much trouble!"

A moment later, Harry's mom returns with a broom and dust pan. She begins to clean up the broken vase, when Harry nervously asks, "Do you think we can fix it?"

"I don't know," she replies. "We can try, but it will never be the same."

"Oh...and what about us?" Harry gulps, then whispers, "Do you still...trust me?"

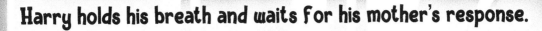

Harry holds his breath and waits for his mother's response.

"Harry, I'm not going to lie to you. I am upset that you broke the rule about running in the house and broke my vase."

"But I am happy you chose to tell me the truth. By being honest, you have shown me how much you're growing up into a respectful young man, and I am proud of you."

"Come on. Let's go to the kitchen and see if we can fix the vase. Maybe...you can even have a cookie."

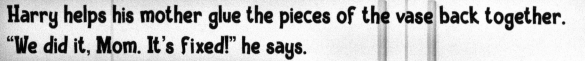
Harry helps his mother glue the pieces of the vase back together.
"We did it, Mom. It's fixed!" he says.

"PERFECT!" she responds. "And it looks even better now with the sparkly gold glue we had, too. Gives it a NEW artistic flair, I think."

"ME TOO!"
Harry tells her.

"Oh...After I finish my cookies, may I be excused to play with my friends? I promise I'll walk."

"Of course."

"**YIPPEE!**" Harry shouts with glee and **WALKS** out of the kitchen.

Remember, if your parents tell you not to run through the house, it's probably for a good reason.

They don't want you to get hurt or break something important like my mom's favorite vase.

Well, I've got to go! See you next time!

Oh...Don't forget, to collect all our adventures and to join my club visit:
www.AdventuresofHarryandFriends.com

More to come...

CPSIA information can be obtained
at www.ICGtesting.com
Printed in the USA
BVHW021403290322
632750BV00005B/430